Time & Again
Life Poems

Nigel Linacre

Time & Again
Life Poems

Nigel Linacre

ISBN: 9781079913118
nigel@nigellinacre.com
July 2019

Contents

80. III Revelation

1. A Gift

If every moment was a gift
In which you had the chance to lift
The spirits of each life you touch
Say what could matter half as much

For every moment you let fly
Without greeting each passer-by
No word, no look, no silent wish
Was no more than an empty dish

Each instant that you did not see
The life in you and me and thee
Instead with mind preoccupied
You thought, and then the moment died

You would yet see paradise
If you could look with fresher eyes
Let go of all the thoughts that stray
And we will write another play

2. Love knows love

Let us not darken this day
Or each and any instant slay
But to this now attention pay
For this is life in every way

You seek the answer that is clear
But never see that it's right here
You're blinded by a crippling fear
And cannot feel the love that's near

Love knows love and knows no other
A critic could become a brother
The key is not to change another
But yourself become the lover

You know this all will soon be gone
And you may see your works outshone
But know your love may ripple on
The work of love is never done

3. Temporal Triptych

4. I Once upon a time

Before the beginning, the start of it all
There wasn't one breath, and nothing to call
Life knew not itself, and there was no sense
Not one thing could be, not even suspense

From voidless void flew all that would be
Unheard noise, fire nothing could see
The parts flung apart, before they were old
Into dimension, where nothing would hold

Time started to tick, but hid its intent
Bringing each moment, each instant that went
Swallowing life, then birthing the next
Life and death flexed, time stilled the context

The future imagined, a creature of mind
Past held for longer, by new life confined
Framing the whole in familiar contours
Of deep rutted paths and repetitive tours

The end cannot be, nor ever be known
For in each moment, the next step is sown
Then after it all, comes yet one more part
A place that's in time, a place of the heart

5. II The present

The present persists, but is easily missed
Becoming the past, where memories last
Leaving impressions of serial sessions
Where presence goes, no-one yet knows

The present insists, it's here and it is
A bridge from back then to an unformed when
It's the reality, free from all fantasy
But when it is seen, it already has been

The present resists, it already is
No change can be made, its pattern is laid
Accept this present, for here we frequent
Too fast it has gone, yet we carry on

The present consists, of all that now is
Yet must be empty, save for what would be
No sound or movement, no time is misspent
Remaining wrapped, yet never untapped

The present persists, enigma it is
A void of no thing, and yet everything
Hidden in here is the key to it all
When else could we be? No place at all

6. III Into infinity

Eternity expresses self in change
Which being changed, is not eternal
Infinity finds form in finity
Inhabiting a fraction of its range

The constant comes alive in variety
Where affected, vibrates inconstantly
Life gains its sharpness in its very end
As life begets death, begets life and death

And so one thing has become another
Which is as it must be and yet be not
Still where is the hand if not in glove?
Which might be seen within, if not above

The noisome sense not the eternal hush
The finite feels not the infinite chord
The inconstant miss the constant beat
And the living live in the light of death

The self silently searches for the self
As a shadow dances with a shadow
Enjoying the particularities of life
Pirouetting then falling into infinity

7. Code of life

The path of life is yours to walk
If you can step beyond the talk

The game of life is yours to win
If you can look outside and in

The stuff of life is yours to gain
If you treat nothing with disdain

The cares of life are yours to lose
If you believe and if you choose

The way of life is yours to find
If you can step outside the mind

The love of life is yours to share
If you will open-hearted dare

The code of life is yours to know
If to the unknown you will go

8. Majesty

If you could hear and taste and see
How marvellous would this life be

If you could also smell and touch
Might life itself become too much

If you had arms and legs and hands
You would stride across these lands

If you could self-reflect and think
Such thoughts divine you would then drink

If you could now choose this life's path
You would at fickle fate but laugh

But you now have all this I see
A life of blessed majesty!

9. Womb to tomb

Born into this world from womb
Return much later to the tomb
The walls of life are plain to see
A frame for earthly symmetry

The rhythmic breath upon this sphere
The days and nights and seasons clear
Make this world seem oh so real
But something else it does conceal

We're living in the world of dreams
Held captive by the gold that gleams
Absorbed in doing and having more
We've lost all sense of what life's for

And something else is going on
That tells me that we don't belong
Like aliens we visit here
Trying to find a course to steer

Before the womb, beyond the tomb

Inhabiting another room
A ticket to the world material
Returning journey to ethereal

But even so, while you are here
You could yet become the seer
That sees beyond the world of shades
Rejoice in hope of sunlit glades

10. Back here

On waking it is all too clear
That I am once again back here
Might I have played another part
If dawn had brought a different start

Let go of every error that
Forgotten is no longer fact
The source of every hidden shame
All gone for this was just a game

But if this life I do let go
To wake as one I don't yet know
The one that brought this all about
Would still remain with every doubt

For while I'll wear a different mask
It is still me and so the task
Is here and it is to transform
This living thing beyond the norm

To shed the skin that I'm stuck in
And let the glory shine within
The radiant glorious king of light
A greater truth of which to write

11. Awakening

It seemed as tho' my soul woke up
And came to earth with me to sup
At first it seemed so strange to me
The most amazing energy

A silent visitor to my space
Would disappear with just a trace
Of direction that did feel so pure
A peace that somehow did endure

At first it felt just gently blessed
Perhaps there was a simple test
An option that might come and stay
And bring alive another day

But then it was I came to see
The soul that was awake in me
From slumber missing the divine
Imagining this earth was mine

Complete surrender to the soul
Becomes the only way to whole

The sublimation of who was
Of suffering often most the cause

Old self enveloped in the new
Combines informing someone who
Let's go the old, brings in the true
In time to come, we live anew

12. Confession

In truth I have for you no blame
For it turns out we're both the same
And I have learned I must accept
All that in others I'd reject
For all along it was in me
I could not and I would not see
A game of falsity I played
My rendezvous with truth delayed

It would have cut me like a sword
Or so I thought looking toward
I hid within a veil of lies
Each one designed to hide the skies
Of all that I had yet to know
My truth I held that it was so
So stayed within my soft cocoon
Where life would find me all too soon

I thought that I had found the way
Tho' what it was I couldn't say.
And I was better, for I walked
Although in truth I mostly talked

But now I see 'twas I who's stuck
Relying 'til this time on luck
Avoiding what was not my friend
That might have caused my ways to bend

What can I say in my defence?
Now that I see there was offence
My words and acts that I relied
Were nothing more than empty pride
I had the truth I knew for certain
But could not see behind the curtain
Nor having seen could look beyond
Nor seek within a deeper bond

But spirit would yet come for me
For it would help me feel and see
Yet tho' it gave me every chance
To rise above this earthly dance
I was the poorest student yet
Who quickly would all this forget
Preferring of this life to drink
Then make a little time to think

My thoughts kept going, round and round

As tho' they spun up from the ground
Their logic built on premises
A chance to grab life's promises
But almost every thought I had
Good, indifferent or bad
Was judged on how it would me serve
So help me get what I deserve

I yearned to get beyond the self
But this was also for myself
Another trick of what was me
To justify what it would be
I tried to push that self away
But found it stayed here anyway
It pressed me and the two confused
And so such change it did refuse

I had to drag it to the light
Not so that we would have to fight
But just to see it was this shell
That had been giving me such hell
And let it know 'twould be OK
There were no words it had to say
No explanations must be given

For it in truth was now forgiven

The self I knew of yesterday
I will let go, it falls away
This loss I easily conceal
For it was never, ever real.
It must in time be crucified
That is the way the old self died
For you must let the new self grow
Tho' it's not anyone you know.

It feels like there's a God within
That brings about an end to sin
But first you must turn off the noise
That meeting with divine destroys
You might within the silence find
A way out of this mortal mind
The one you thought you always knew
That broken self to which we're true

If this is not a path you know
The good news is you've far to go
There may be much that you have planned
But even more to understand

You wouldn't such a path have taken
If you weren't so much mistaken
Consider that you do not know
Who you are or where you'll go
This life, this glorious mystery
Unseen by all who cannot see
Save things already for their use
The stuff of life they don't refuse
Themselves another thing to do
Becoming old what once was new
The life flies by without a look
At what this is, for they mistook

The magic for a tool to bend
To goals that faded in the end
The sadness is the life was missed
They'd much to do, they did insist
But it was mostly getting stuff
That's what they thought would be enough
The hidden goal to gain position
Preferred to any sense of mission

Then vital this to justify
No talk of death or even why

The imminent and total loss
Of all that's gained whatever cost
Must be averted or denied
With eyes closed to the end of ride
We must maintain this edifice
Before we pay whatever price

The game that most of us still play
Which won't persist, it ends one day
Could be replaced by something great
I tell you now it's not too late
The proof is you exist at all
Tho' some would say you've had a fall
This is the time you can arise
On your old self, spring a surprise

Let go of every melodrama
Let slip a bigger panorama
The battle of your soul enjoined
Success in a new mint be coined
The tools are peace and just submission
Within that space a perfect mission
All that you would come to be
Awaits you now, for you are free

---

13. One more day

It looks like I've another day
What will I hear, what will I say
A chance to see this world anew
What will I think, what will I do

Needing to rise and go about
While in my mind a quiet shout
Allowing just the briefest pause
Opening and closing doors

Why do I think things will go wrong
Once I am up, it won't take long
Before my mind is filled with worry
It makes me see the world all blurry

True bad things haven't happened yet
But it remains an unknown bet
I must try to prevent a loss
At least not let myself get cross

I know well this limiting feeling

It quickly sends my mind a-reeling
But how to have a better idea
When as yet the day's not clear

I could imagine a great day
Unlikely as that seems today
Try as I might to start to see it
It unravels bit by bit

Still I see I have to find
Another way to change my mind
To get myself to a great place
Build some future on that base

Perhaps the future holds the key
To not thinking so much of me
But seek to find a glorious mission
To which I'd give a great intention

That justifies the rest of life
To lessen trouble, banish strife
In which I put the others first
Not myself better or even worse

Could I find some liberation
From obsessing about station
Not need to be recognised
And see this day with open eyes

It looks like I've another day
What will I hear what will I say
A chance to see this world anew
What will I say what will I do?

14. Morning

I feel life as it starts to rise
Once more tho' with still tired eyes
Sweet sleep and dreams where our time flies
Dismissed, dispersed by day's sunrise

The dreams that had all night felt real
Which came and went and would reveal
Those hopes and fears, now lie concealed
The morning light brings life to heel

Beyond the bed, the room around
Which listens hard for any sound
Attuned to threat upon this ground
That might this peaceful bed surround

The arms, the legs, do turn once more
The bed supports, no need to soar
Wondering not what this is for
The world out there won't be ignored

What bed is this, what must be done

Err long while this day is still young
What tasks from yesterday undone
That soon will have me on the run

Where, when, how, who and what to do
Some tasks and asks, so many new
I cannot stay but must come to
It's time to fly, to live anew

15. Gladden

Gladden each heart, live this whole day
Don't hesitate, for it won't stay
Don't hold life back, nothing you lack
When you just give, find how to live

All that you see, won't make you free
Chains of the mind, you must unbind
You like to do, seek first a clue
Find how to be, here is the key

All that is gone, won't make you one
For what's to come, find a new drum
You could create, beyond your fate
It's time to see, who you could be

You could be whole, one with your soul
If you would hear, and then let steer
The wisdom within, where to begin
Before you know, let life be so

16. Too late

It is too early in the day
To tell a truth I cannot say
To those who do not seek the way
And think that this is where they'll stay

You say that there is naught to know
And hope that you won't need to go
But tho' you may not see what's so
The truth will catch you, fast or slow

My friend he disappeared last week
His heart turned out to be too weak
We've no more time for truths to speak
His parting leaves me feeling bleak

It may be later than you think
To find that truth from which you shrink
And there may scarce be time to blink
For you to find in life a link

Suppose that all of this is real
You cannot from the whole conceal

It may not matter how you feel
Sooner or later, time to kneel

17. Walk on

The keys to life aren't hard to find
If you will discipline your mind
Which like an imbecile will natter
Endless hours of useless chatter

The love of life becomes an art
If you will open up your heart
Start by breathing nice and slow
Your heart is ready, on you go

The point of life will be quite clear
When you can free the self from fear
No need to maintain old defences
Steadily dropping life's pretences

The path of life is here right now
And you must walk it anyhow
The choice to stay asleep or wake
As you new dreams do undertake

18. Oh, great

Who are you not to be great?
You think this a matter of fate
The risk is the time gets too late
It's time to try another gate

You're sure that you don't want to fail
Then have to tell a sadder tale
So still before the future quail,
This thinking keeps you in a jail

The greater loss, not to take wing
Find you can fly, so please begin
To look outside and venture in
A life that missed, might be a sin

For now it's time to venture out
A life not whispered, you can shout
You could figure this whole thing out
This is what life is all about

19. Ticking clock

Why youngster, tell me, what's your goal?
What would you build before you're old?
What need do you have for control?
What is it that would make you whole?

What will you do, and what rules break?
What difference then will your life make?
What's in this life for which you ache?
What is the path your life will take?

While some will tell you what to do
And mean to lure you with things new
And try to make you join their crew
But only to yourself be true

Suppose your life on earth is here
To make something important clear
With any luck you've many a year
The clock is ticking, time to steer

20. Perfect day

Tired eyes that sting to earth's sunrise
Cool air that is the lung's surprise
Fog-filled the head upon the bed
The day's arrived with gentle dread

Sleep had brought a hard-earned pause
The day no longer reached its claws
The dreams since slipped away from mind
A way to meet the day to find

Lie, sit, stand, walk into morning
Seek a sense of what is dawning
What could this new day be about
What must be done, when to go out?

As mind and body come to terms
And days' unbidden stark returns
Serve up the uncompleted tasks
Plus unforeseeable new asks

Find a place to get some stillness
Or settle into the day's illness

If this could be a perfect day
What would be done, what would we say?

21. Dawn chorus

Shall I greet each brand new day
As tho it has something to say
From dawn to dusk I'll carry on
For it must be my companion

I feel the sun upon my face
A gentle breeze of it a trace
Of doubt careering in my mind
What must I do, what must I find

What choices must I make today
Who must I see, what must I say
But first instead a moment's pause
To be someone without a cause

To hear the chorus of the birds
That lift my spirits without words
The earth that I will walk upon
That calls until summer has gone

With just a shorter pause at night

Where I await returning light
Lost within my dreams' surmise
Where I await the next sunrise

22. Until samsara

What must be done before we go
Along the path that we don't know
Beyond the stuff of maintenance
Of this and that and will you dance

Something somewhere calling you
To greater knowing of what's true
Some simple reason to have come
A way of knowing it's been done

A method found for all of this
The basic point of all that is
A chance to fleetingly express
The possibilities of yes

Walking with floating karma
Serving a deeper dharma
The sublimation of the self
Samsara becomes what else?

23. Ebb and flow

You don't know who you're born to be
In future that you cannot see
But if you could see each instant
The future we could not invent

Tho' we would know what's going on
We'd live our lives in a prison
Leaving us stuck with certain fate
In which no room to have debate

We must with life's ebb and flow
Chart a course that we don't know
We may adjust for each high tide
But we must presently abide

Here's to perpetual ignorance
That leaves us room for earthly dance
While it cannot be made our own
We'll move to destiny unknown

24. The Spiral

25. I In house

Existing is a slight surprise
A riddle just before the eyes
A space to speak, to sing and shout
To think deep thoughts or just hang out
As tho' a half-forgotten plot
Foresaw this, that and what-not
But left a hanging rail of ties
And little room to improvise

Existing is a slight surprise
Perhaps that's it, this life, the prize
Stops us short to breathe once more
And notice walls, ceiling and floor
This moment, this and yet another
Filled with sound and smell and colour
Passed by in a blur of stuff
And wondering if this is enough

Existing is a slight surprise
Next seen thru slightly aged eyes
The ups and downs of life contrast
Hiding the whole until the last
Joy and tragedy dance so slow

Embracing the other each to know
Life and death this patchwork play
On guest house earth for now we stay

26. II In decision

One moment this and every one
That came to be and slide beyond
Brightly flashing, suddenly falling
Into a skip of what once was.
The light went out and ran about
Looking for rays that would not dim
Waiting for her or was it for him
A secret to tell all in all

You came and you were also here
Who you were was not so clear
Something, you know there was something
There was a time when we were here
One day I will or I would have
And you may say that I should have
My mind a sea of indecision
Lacking in necessary precision

The mind jabbers through another turn
Wondering how and what it will earn
Looking for an oft' repeated role
Knowing none will make it whole

Another day slides quickly by
Only occasionally asking why
Life irresistibly occurring
Something deep within us stirring

27. Ill Imperfect

In the perfect life there's nothing to do
No need for me, no need for you.
If perfect contains the imperfect path
At imperfections we may laugh.
The unbeaten track is what's worth walking
Sometimes digressing, dawdling, talking
The rest distractions, movement to factions
While comforting thoughts delay our actions

But where is this path, where does it begin?
Your feet cannot find it, for it is within
The imperfect path is the path you are on
When you try to move off it, it just carries on
It's the path you are walking wherever you are
It will carry you near, it will carry you far
But however you work on your fears and fumbles
You'll encounter no shore to the sea of troubles

For the imperfect path is the path of loss
Discovering that you are not the boss
The journey it turns out is about letting go
Of the self you were and once did know

As that 'you' disappears, the conduit of fears
A cause of excitement and so many tears
An emergent self comes into its own
Heard on the path, it welcomes you home

28. Mystery

You who've been born in mystery
But cannot see you breathe and be
You seek some strong security
Its price is less reality

You know this life is sadly short
But you avoid this unjust tort
Believe life's riches you have bought
On life's dilemma you are caught

You live your life in constant tension
While holding on with apprehension
Of deeper quest there is no mention
You dream of living on a pension

You know that you must suffer loss
But brush on life the latest gloss
At other people you get cross
While grasping life as candy floss

You strive to focus on your gain
And if you can avoid the pain

From all life's trials you'd abstain
But will not walk this way again

Do come with me it's time to sup
And tho' you seek a sweeter cup
I will not take you for a pup
But whisper that the game is up

29. Doing time

The prison bars tho' far too strong
Do comfort me that I belong
All four walls so flat and cool
They hold within this helpless fool

There's room within the walls to play
A range of games enough to stay
And live a little life of sorts
Alternating one's and noughts

Between the bars is something green
A life that might in time be seen
Say better not to see at all
Instead embracing mankind's fall

What if the walls are in my mind
The truths beyond are hard to find
The door itself may be ajar
But I won't wonder very far

30. Doorway

This human life takes many forms
Billions of people with their norms
Millions more species fast revolve
As we together all evolve

Beyond this earth light years away
Millions of stars light the Milky way
We see so little of the magic
Obsessed on our own lives tragic

Some earthly humans sense there's more
Then try to knock at heaven's door
While the wish for worldly pleasure
We enjoy with greater measure

Mind and matter here conjoined
Love and life in language coined
Ever more mystery to explore
But will we ever find the door?

31. Tracing dreams

This moment this and every one
That ever was has been and gone
The instant of this perfect now
A moment's pause will not allow
Each fragment that has yet to be
We do not see it makes us free

For we who must be born and die
Confined by earth and sea and sky
Can in imagination soar
That makes invisible each door
Then fly for better dreams await
Those who'd escape a worldly fate

Let's pass beyond the land of fears
Let go your hold, let flow the tears
It's time to find that better place
Where heaven's dreams we dare to trace
Go there today, don't waste a day
The truth to find, there is a way

32. One part

On seeing all the stages
And the turning of the pages
The this and that, they just won't do
They scarcely can describe what's true

You heart it aches for gentle healing
A deeper kind of meaning
A time to swim with perfect flow
An end to being on the go

A way to be that's far more whole
Then other travellers console
Embrace the joy and sadness too
Infuse with love all that you do

A greater kind of being
You're quite unused to seeing
From which you've mostly been apart
But of which you remain a part

33. Debutant

You never will get it all done
The work, the dreams, the words, the fun
Whatever tasks you have begun
It feels the whole thing's on the run
Where you must live a life undone
With ne'er a final victory won

It turns out that a life complete
While feeling good and looking neat
From you the rest of life would cheat
For then at best you'd oft' repeat
Whatever had been your best feat
Without fresh challenge, cruel defeat

To think of great things you can do
To dream of thrills of struggles new
Do not give in, think not you're through
The hardest tasks come to make you
The unknown star, somebody who
Has yet to make their next debut

34. Lost identity

Before its birth I lost itself
And settled then for something else
A fraction of its unformed glory
Which then became a timebound story

Finding self in mind and body
It said that I must be somebody
I tell you who this is you see
The somebody you see is me

Mind-body sought identity
Not wanting to be fantasy
It had a sense of self to feed
But found itself always in need

It keenly felt something missing
And sought to get it by amassing
Food and clothes and rooms and houses
Sometimes even others' spouses

Perpetual wanting thus remained
Ever from inner life abstained
It did not matter where it went
A better life could not invent

35. Self undone

They searched for some significance
But gave few things a second glance
They wanted an impact to make
At least not make a big mistake
They hoped to find more than chance
A life in which we all advance

A meaning that they could live by
A God that wasn't in the sky
A way to live along with nature
Seeing beauty in a picture
But most of life was in a rush
They seldom saw or felt deep hush

They struggled to the left and right
Not seeing any kind of light
Focused on what they could earn
And if it helped what they would learn
Wishing sometime to overcome
The world, the self was left undone

36. Throw the dice

The fear that always stayed in me
That never would quite let me free
That followed me from dawn to dusk
That told me that I always must
Take the safe route, the trodden way
Be careful lest they'd laugh and say
He tried, he failed and tho' he sailed
He never really had life nailed

The thing that now I most regret
Was where I would not willing bet
Then let life do its best and worse
Throw down the dice, whatever course
Let them then say he lived, he tried
He had a go, before he died
He left the field resources spent
Not wondering where this life went

37. Time frame

The precious moments, every one,
Which hurry through us, then are gone,
So we are left to soldier on
Expressing more to live upon;
Without whose onward march in time
We have no path on which to climb,
No way to guide us to our prime
To miss that mark would be a crime.

Each moment comes as fast as goes
Its destination no one knows;
Was this the future that we chose
How does this work do you suppose?
If time itself would set us free
Then there could be no you or me
The truth is here for us to see
Time binds us to our destiny.

38. Unsaid

We know that it is not our way
To talk of feelings which must stay
Hid deep inside and far away
Things unsaid from yesterday

Here there might be a chance to feel
And from our thoughts a moment steal
Where we could finally be real
And in that moment friendship seal

Let go of all from elsewhere sent
Forget the past and where it went
But in delightful now frequent
And we shall find a steep ascent

For here's the risk and here's the pace
Surrendering history without trace
A story we have yet to face
The boundaries of infinite space

39. Upon the waves

The risk of life that you might fail
To catch a wind from here and sail
To stay on this familiar shore
Then wonder what it was all for

For every life must catch the tide
If this would be a worthwhile ride
Check now the hour of the shoreline
There's little time to life refine

Abandon safety of firm ground
The sea must all our lives surround
The transformation that we seek
Is onc of loss before we speak

Beyond the undulating waves
That rise and fall each soul who braves
The terror of the loss of similar
A song is sung at once familiar

But you could hear it's echo now
Beyond the noises you allow

That make you tack that way and this
The glorious unknown synthesis

40. Nafikiri, nafariki

Nafikiri, nafariki
Lakini sijui ni lini
Nafikiri, nafariki
Lakini sitangoja kito
Nitaishi maisha leo
Nikifikiri nitafariki
Lakini sitangoja kifo
Nitaishi maisha leo

Written in Swahili, translated as follows:

I think I will die
But I don't know when
I think I am dying
But I am not waiting for death
I will live today
Knowing that I will die
But I will not wait for death
I will live life today

41. Thin air

When life makes no sense
And challenges feel immense,
When your body is tense
And your mind feels decidedly dense,
It is time to abandon pretence
Of knowing what, where and whence

There's a time to endure
Uncertainty's part of the tour
Let your mind become more pure
Imagine that you feel secure
Start to see a solution's contour
You'll find a way thru this for sure

You look for solutions out there
A common belief to be fair
You won't find them there anywhere
Instead be relaxed, without care
You may find answers true and fair
Floating as tho' in thin air

42. Beyond the dream

The night cannot keep going on
The dawn must arrive afore long
It seems that things keep going wrong
Such darkness feels ever so strong

The time comes that I must awake
When still there will be my mistake
More problems it seems I must take
With consequences that must break

Why is it that I have free will
Prefer to do the good than ill
Small errors in life mean that still
Of failure I've had of my fill

The sadness must me overwhelm
Someone will be found to condemn
But I find myself still at the helm
Awakening in this dark realm

My hope that one day it won't seem
It's real but a very strange scheme

The darkness by the light redeemed
Oh let me waken from this dream

43. On loan

What is this life if not ours?
Not one of these millions of hours
Nor even our manifest powers

What if this life's just on loan?
A chance to reach worlds unknown
In which destiny may be sown

What if this life is too short?
To do all we feel that we ought
In which too late we are taught

What if this life is for real?
In which there is nothing concealed
Except by a veil that we feel

What if we could yet surprise?
And see life with unblinkered eyes
Might we yet find the greatest surprise?

44. Tell me why

Imagine you truly exist
And for all these years persist
But almost never wonder why
We have earth, sea, land and sky

Instead we lose ourselves in function
Navigating each new junction
We have time for what takes time
Seldom encounter the sublime

We do not know where we come from
Or where we'll go when life is done
The daily things that take our eyes
The dramas of the lows and highs

The patterns of life we repeat
We work with hands we walk with feet
But here's a question not too small
Why is there anything at all?

45. Time drags

Time has carried us far along
Each summer would go on and on
A childhood that is now long gone
With each year's ending we grew strong

The changing of an adolescent
The fleeting nature of the present
The loss of life we can't prevent
The adult life we must invent

The surge, the rush to adulthood
The need to work whatever mood
Less time to dream of what we would
Constrained by life to what we could

A life with family that ages
Children helped through all the stages
Occasionally flying into rages
Life turns another of its pages

So much of it was such a blur
Fixed to a path without demur
Then wonder what it was all for

If there's still time to make a stir

At last I find a flat plateau
No need right here for yes or no
Life feels complete, it is just so
Time was the friend, but now the foe

For time is short and crowds around
The finite nature of all ground
The search for meaning not yet found
This blessed time won't be unwound

We'd slowly go make time to mend
Then dawdle here and not descend
To future that we would not send
Yet time drags us towards its end

46. Prize

Why the surprise, life is the prize
It is now yours, and yours the course
No need to claim, but play the game
Step into role, you won't feel whole
But sense the flow that helps you go
From part to part, life as an art

And in each place, you leave a trace
Of who you are and see how far
You can create, but set no date
For who you'll be or what you'll see
Let life evolve and it will solve
Creating anew as you choose to

Knowing what cost will all be lost
Freed from defence, and slight offence
No feed for fame, no need to blame
No longer stuck, let go the muck
You are now known, as life is sown
Open your eyes, life is the prize

47. Rewind

Most of this life you have held fast
To once and now familiar cast
Attaching to your views steadfast
Not knowing 'til the very last
That every thought was in your past

The magic of each moment spent
Thinking what you could prevent
"A problem, will they soon relent?"
Once it was here, too fast it went
Too bad you missed its full extent

48. Tempo

I know just what I have to do
To make this life as someone new
To dream the dreams of what will be
Then from this empty self I'll flee

This version is but temporary
Our husks do hide both you and me
Don't fix yourself to what is spent
Instead this life let's reinvent

The reasons we'd find to complain
The words and deeds we can't explain
But first embrace the life in all
As spirit loves the physical

Once we've accepted all this stuff
Discovered that there's quite enough
From worldly things we can transcend
Then realize that's not the end

49. Return

Just beyond the day to day
A land of beauty not of clay
A place of peace come what may
For seeing in a different way

Illusions that I suffer here
When I'm there are nowhere near
Living and loving begin to cohere
Truth becoming crystal clear

You could go there anytime
And encounter the sublime

But to that world I must return
For here is where I work and earn
And try and fail and sometimes learn
Still there is where to go I yearn

There is where I get my fuel
And remember life's not dual
Even tho' it oft' seems cruel
Of Heaven's staircase it's the newel

50. Running aground

Something is chasing me but I can't see
Who or what or where it might be
For all of life it's driven me
Few were the moments not at sea

It pushed me forward and held me back
It might be in front and it might attack
So much of life I've felt so stuck
And then deduced it was my luck

Throughout it all I've stayed ahead
Save when it grabbed me in my bed
I lost the path when fixed by fear
No other motivation was that clear

There must come time to turn around
For just one moment stand my ground
It can't be fought it's far too strong
It made me feel I'm in the wrong

At last a way to turn my face
Deciding I'd no longer race

It turns out that the fear I see
Is nothing more than part of me

51. Too sweet

The happiness I do not seek
For it is far too sickly sweet
The steadiness of an even path
Predictable from life to death

That can't be it, it's not the deal
Which heaven's sake is how I feel
Give me the path of love and loss
And let me feel that I'm the boss

I'll make mistakes and hope for breaks
And try to give it what it takes
I'll take the pain and hope for gain
That I may one day life explain

Give me contrast that will not last
And let me move on from each past
For every challenge I survive
Reminds me that I'm still alive

52. Shame game

Without a sense of deepest shame
What need have we to play the game
To live, to strive, to come alive
To see these moments, not the same

Each one is birthed in fresh desire
That forces us here us to enquire
What path, what choice, we could rejoice
That finds within a deeper fire

Each horror from which we did turn
That gave us one more chance to spurn
The darker path, the mask, the wrath
Now choosing not the light to burn

Throughout our lives we all have failed
To feel the winds that would have sailed
The waves, the tides, the shore of love
In breathing it may be unveiled

Love the darkness, make no plea
But find the mind of liberty

No fight, no right, just be the light
That loves in all eternity

53. Step into unknown

What to do when you don’t know
Perhaps the only way to go
Means stepping into the unknown
Where you may meet what you have sown

Refer to what you say you know
Thinking you know that it is so
This life’s too dull to stick to known
Supposing anything’s your own!

Then cast all certitude aside
Hold on make this a glorious ride
Rejoice that there is much to know
For where it takes you, you don’t know

54. Shielded

Beyond this mess of life, I know
That something in me still does grow
It can't be seen and rarely speaks
But may be felt by she who seeks

Occluded by the noise and stress
And hard to reach when in distress
It may have never left my side
Hidden from sight and deep inside

It's strange that I so little reach
The one who would me all things teach
Feeling the pull of outward senses
I've tried myself to jump life's fences

It's been perplexing comedy
In which my first thought's often me
Yet there remains beside me still
That which my own life would fill

I've done enough to make it spurn
And from this being ever turn

Yet for its life I would all yield
My soul, defender and my shield

55. Dreamer

The dreams that in time passed me by
I saw emblazoned 'cross the sky
But then a cloud occluded eye
I let slip the reason why

Instead and as the clouds did form
I thought they did portend a storm
And shrivelling back towards the norm
Died the idea that would reform

Perhaps the path was safe and clear
I might have found a way to steer
But I surrendered to the fear
No date with destiny drew near

Watch what floats across your mind
For there a great dream you may find
It could be with your life entwined
Do not leave your dreams behind

56. Evening

Lying still in bed this night
Feeling the fading of the light
No urge remains for fight or fright
With almost no more words to write

All that I had upon this day
I must let go, nothing can stay
While what I tried to do this day's
Now in the past where it decays

Each task that I had sought to do
Had seemed important, often new
The work that I had felt was due
All falls away from current view

Paths that I have not yet taken
Which in time may prove mistaken
Might somewhere in me awaken
First, it's time for sleep unshaken

I must surrender all that seems
So vital in my many schemes

And let dissolve all of life's themes
While sinking into fleeting dreams

57. Befriending fear

Fear is the key that I now see
It tries to say something to me
But every time from it I shrink
There's no new truth that I can drink

I thought throughout it was my foe
And where it went, I could not go
I had that darkness to escape
Tho' never could quite see the shape

The fear so often held me back
There must be something that I lack
And to myself could not be true
I'll seek the fear near me and you

So I would try to meet at last
Before this carrier 'gain flies past
Here's truth that I could never see
For now I find the fear's in me

If all concerns, I could have met
Then I would have but no regret
This life then lived without disguise

Which I'd have seen with fearless eyes

The moment that you next sense fear
Bid it tarry, stay right here
Look with love upon the foe
And you will change the world you know

58. Something missing

Something is whispering but isn't being heard
Something so important that is constantly deferred
The noise of the world would drown the rest out
But you see the thing is, the soul won't shout

Something is missing but you can't say what it is
Something that will call to you and also give you peace
The sights of the world would always fill your eyes
But if you ever meet the soul, you'd be in for a surprise

Something is loving you whatever time and place
There is no obstacle preventing its embrace
The wants of the world would keep you in their grasp
But if you get to know the soul you will gasp

Something is helping and stays ready to assist
Call out to it and it will not resist
The things of the world you may want it to bring
But walk with the soul and your wish is to sing

There's something in life that cannot be found
By seeking here and there and everywhere around
Instead of all that you must go into the deep
Better explore before you fall asleep

59. Sweet surprise

Every creature that draws breath
Must sometime soon encounter death
Each moment that is born and dies
Would let another bring surprise

Every thing that we would know
Walked before the way we go
That we might come in time to see
A way to do, a place to be

Every act where we define
Within eternity's sweet wine
The fragment held within our grasp
Missing the whole, we do not gasp

Every moment flickering fast
Carrying this impermanent cast
We play with this reality
While also yearning to be me

We seek within the world romance
But hardly know we're in a trance
One day we may from dreams awake
In death another life to make

60. Son gone

Our son as was, has been and gone
Became a man and soldiers on
No longer seeks or wants our aid
Seeking his own way to be paid

He treats his life like it's his own
And seldom calls us on the phone
Well that's all fine but we're bereft
There's been a hole since he has left

From time to time we reconnect
But somehow we do still expect
To see the boy who once was ours
But now confined to our memoirs

The influence that we once had
Has all now gone for good or bad
He cannot hear his mum or dad
They were just parents he once had

61. Strangers to life

Life the greatest mystery
Open your eyes and you will see
The glory of this very day
Where you live and hide and play

It's true you worry and you fret
Numb emotions and regret.
The majesty and ecstasy
Are strangers to your life I see

The mask you wear upon your face
I see behind and there's a trace
Of love behind the fear of shame
But know that we are all the same

Fear you have harboured since a child
Suppressing it to not grow wild
Was there in all you thought were strangers
Wherefrom you imagined dangers

It's time to strip away pretence
And venture to the new lands whence
The fog of fear has lifted clear

The course of love is how you steer

Get up for you have been in trance
Asleep where you had left to chance
The outcomes of this vital realm
So grasp the wheel, you have the helm

Now flee your cage there is no door
Nor bar you need imagine more
The thoughts that said you weren't enough
Throw them away, redundant stuff

The stage is yours not to escape
Nor need to hide behind a cape
But see perfection, here we are
Embracing love upon a star

62. Beauty unseen

The stress descending like a cloud
Which surrounds me like a crowd
That would not hear a shout out loud
Herein no gentleness allowed

Tired eyes, my tissue dries
Legs tired from too many tries
A head no longer wise
Somewhere inside me something cries

There was a time life did impress
But what it does now is depress
These hopes and fears I can't address
It's time to take a short recess

I've lost the sense of majesty
Kept thinking all of this was me
The beauty I have yet to see
Would strip me of my misery

63. Love and light

Beyond this world, beyond it all
Is nothing that I can recall
Save for a source of love and light
That fast eclipses every fight

It lifts me up and would transform
It takes me way beyond the norm
These feet of clay this heart of stone
No longer are they mine to own

I see what I had never seen
No longer am I who I've been
The toys of yesterday have gone
The joys of the old life outshone

To worlds beyond I must return
They feed my soul, this world would burn
Yet having been there I can bring
Something that in me does sing

The ventures of this world all told
Are really something to behold

But greater ventures would await
Those who'll escape this earthly fate

64. Silence spoken

Time was that I would greet each morn
As an adventure being born
Each even hour as a fresh gift
That could in time my spirits lift
I'd seek to greet each life I touched
As tho' it mattered very much

She said her partner had been killed
We stood together as we welled
She said that I should not be kind
I did not want to pain be blind
How ghastly, awful, but no word
Would tragedy make less absurd

There was no place for happiness
Where stood a gnawing tenderness
That stripped away the smiles, the gaze
And offered nothing to replace
The terror of our fates unknown
In the silence somehow spoken

Happiness now is out of reach
It offers up no way to breach

The smiling inexactitude
Of pleasantries that seem so rude
Avoiding all the pain now felt
At unexpected cards misdealt

Suspend the saccharine of life
And so make pain another wife
The better for this life to feel
Not just pretence but also real
To touch behind all of life’s dross
The joy and pain of love and loss

65. Just beyond

The moment just beyond our deaths
That follows fast the last of breaths
No time remaining for a plan
When we've consumed our mortal span

If we can sense that stage at all
And there is then a name to call
In something like an empty hall
What to say, who would you call?

Hidden away in the hall of regrets
The physical's gone and so it let's
Us fly and dream and carry on
To learn and sing another song

What follows life in such a place
Suspended outside time and space
Perchance a chance to live once more
Would bring us back from evermore

66. Taken

Come take us one, come take us all
Does it matter where we will fall?
Or what we said or who we knew
Or how we lay or yet with who

Come take us one, come take us all
Does it matter where we set stall?
The things we did, the places seen
The posts we held, or who we've been

Come take us one, come take us all
Does it matter, we had it all?
The fun, the food, the stuff we wore
The others' struggles we ignore

Come take us one, come take us all
Does it matter, if this is all?
Work squeezed time and life went by
Thinking of me, friends and what's mine

Come take us one, come take us all
Does it matter, here is a call

This time is drawing to a close
What was important, it soon goes

Come take us one, come take us all
We are ready, that is all

67. Time to embrace

Thank you for being you
And taking the trouble to do
What had to be done
For you were the one
Who helped me to learn as I grew

Thank you for being you
You've had most of life it is true
What a great life it's been
Tho' we've not always seen
The works that you always did do

Thank you for being you
Each remaining day can feel new
A time to embrace
The next part of this space
And find something more that is true

68. Time over

Time was not mine, when I was young
The days were vast, not so much past
Time was my friend, as I grew tall
More strength for me, I would not fall
Time was still here, as life went by
Much to be done, not so much fun
Time was the frame, it would not stop
As I grew old, it would not stop

Time is the thief, that all along
Would say time's up, and now be gone

Life beginning and life ending
Held in paired parentheses
For an uncertain time of being
Where we create hypotheses
Wanting to say something prescient
Over-influenced by sentiment
Trying to understand the drama
Or one's place in all the karma

Time is the thief, that all along

Would say time's up, and now be gone

69. Time to go

It searches the skies
And the ground where life lies
Taking them one at a time
Taking them all
The quick and the tall
Knowing not when or where
Or that life will be fair, just
Knowing one day they must
Hoping it is not to be now
Never sweet, sweet now

Seeking a perpetual deferral
A universal cure all
To avoid the unimaginable
And remain in the physical

Time to go, time to go
Some more time to go
Yet the unexpected
Awaits undetected
You do not know
Where will they go

Still nowhere they know

The uncommon journey
Yet common to us all
We'll say it's not here
And stay our fear of fears
In permanent temperance
A party without partings
Until surprising greetings
Him or her with a card gone
Now we suppose on their own
Or quietly dismembered
But partially remembered
As another generation
Rises and falls
Regrets and then forgets
Until what remains is this sigh

Taking them one at a time
Taking them all
The quick and the tall

70. If I wouldn't

If I would not prevaricate
And leave it to my empty fate
To choose the goal and pick the date
Then I could start to grow

If I would not insist on form
And say that my way is the norm
From time to time create a storm
Then I could start to flow

If I would not say this is it
And analyze life bit by bit
Deciding what is counterfeit
Then I might start to know

If I would not fit life in frame
Until it seems it's all the same
And have no need to seek of fame
Then I might higher aim

If I would not intellectualize
And see this life without mind's eyes

In every moment find surprise
Then I might ever glow

71. Only yesterday

You know only yesterday
Subject to faulty recollection
The good days better than the bad
You'd make tomorrow yesterday
Squeezing it into familiar formation
Like the yesterday you already had

But you could come into today
The moment without information
A place you could always be glad
Where there is nothing you need say
No need to analyse this situation
Think something good or bad

You could create another day
A tomorrow of imagination
In which your dreams are clad
Where everything you say
Can affect that situation
And to the present add

72. Let there be joy

Don't think I'm gone as you go on
With day to day, let this thought stay
Love is the creed, and when you need
Bring me to mind, I'm here you'll find

The joy of life is far too brief
And yet feel me, there is no thief
Between us now, we are somehow
Connected yet, free of regret

It was so fine, in its own way
Yet as it was, I couldn't stay
That time and place we think thereof
And still feel this, the force of love

Let there be joy, amidst the tears
And make a fire of senseless fears
This breath, this life, this glorious fount
Live and be well, make each day count

73. Undreamt dreams

The dreams you have not dreamed
The lives you have not changed
The paths you have not walked
The life you have not lived

That you had thought had all but gone
For failure had become your song
A gentle lowering of expectations
Another range of incantations

The moments you ignored
The times when you were bored
The future then unstored
The dull moments you record

But look around without within
Not so much focus on where you've been
The past is naught but memory
So let it go that you may see

The future's still yours to create
The chapters in the book of fate
Are not all written there is still

The application of your will

The dreams you may yet dream
The lives you can still change
The paths you can yet walk
The life you may yet live

74. Box

I've spent all of my life on the run
And can tell you it's not that much fun
But I can't see the face
Of the one who does chase
Let us trust that it isn't the one

I have found it too easy to blame
As a way of avoiding my shame
For the faults that I see
Are also in me
It turns out that we're all the same

I've discovered it's best to create
When I no longer believe in fate
Each action it's clear
This life can now steer
I'd better get on or be late

I've encountered in life so much fear
When there's been no threat anywhere near
It is so hard to find
A space in the mind
Where a fear won't ever appear

I've put most of life in a box
Stuffed it in & then turned the locks
If I let it come out
Who knows what it may shout
I'm not sure that I could stand the shocks

75. Time was their gift

Time took each one, time took them all
Time was their gift, time brought their fall

It seemed so slow, with years to spare
They had decades, no need for prayer
But on one day, they came to know
Too late that all would have to go

They did not ask, they did not find
So never found real peace of mind
They knew not why they'd come at all
They never even heard the call

Their's was the life, the chance to be
And do and have and hear and see,
And dream of what is not yet seen
Instead of all that might have been

You do not know what time remains
Nor as you age, the aches and pains
So seize this day, tomorrow too
Live, serve and love, it's yours to do

Time took each one, time took them all
Time was their gift, time brought their fall

76. Parting Poem

The joy of being here must pass
The time so great has flown so fast
We'd like to make each moment last
Still smiles must fade into the past

My heart is heavy, I am sad
The face I'd like to show is glad
Or better still, some moments add
But this is all the time we've had

So we who stand and love and gaze
For one more moment to amaze
Wherein my mind this visage stays
While my heart remains suffused with rays

I turn before a tear will fall
It's hard to walk, I just might crawl
But now I hear the future call
Our time is over, that is all

77. Over time

78. I Genesis

The one was all, and all there was
It was what was, and it was not.
Neither beginning nor was there end
There being no being and non-being.
Nothing defined nor yet refined
One was alpha, omega and neither.
There was no lack, nor need nor creed
Nothing to do and nothing for you

From unity such diversity came
Something and nothing in the frame
Matter and anti-matter in balance
Visible and invisible parts in stance
Suns spreading light across the space
Figuring up and down to trace
In this movement there was time
Matter, anti-matter, rhythm and rhyme

A dramatic world of rock and storms
Was born yet lacking in life's forms
Until somehow, life came to be
And fast developed complexity
Seeing its' own existence and pathos

Thinking self separate from all of what was
It knew what it knew, not what it did not
It knew not why and fast forgot

79. II Exodus

The self I see is seen by me
So not the self, if you follow and see
I watch my body and also my mind
But in neither place can the self I find
Wherever I search and in everyone
For the missing piece to carry on
Someone is watching and it just might be
The hidden, invisible silent me

Observe your body and notice change
Monitor your mind as ideas range
Sense the feelings that swiftly arise
Sometimes taking us by surprise
Thought, feeling and body may disappear
Nevertheless, you are still here
The personal baggage that says I'm me
Might be mistaken, I'm starting to see

Sooner or later all that must go
Leaving only the self to know
The dramas that filled our days and nights
The peace that followed so many fights
The growth and decay inbuilt in strife

Were just the coming and going of life
Someone is watching, it’s not someone else
The hidden, invisible, silent self

80. Ill Revelation

The foundation which must at least be true
Is that I am me and you are you
Dispensing with mind, body, emotions
Lies here one going thru the motions
The one who's in every moment been
Reaching out from unseen to seen
A bridge from nothing to time and place
From all that's unformed and into space

Could this unseen be chimera too?
The watching self not the end of you
The day to day being without any ties
Behind the curtain of consciousness lies
Call to it and you will likely hear
Nothing but silence perfectly clear
Still you won't know that it's not there
Looking at you from an unseen lair

Persisting with partial conversation
Not quite sure it's imagination
You may hear another voice arise
And though it remains of uncertain size

The conviction may come that it is real
The rest of the world, a dream you feel
One day you'll wake to the call of your soul
In this time, this life, becoming whole

By the same author

The Great War Poem

I PEACE UNTIL

When Gavrilo Princip raised his gun
He'd no idea what he'd begun.
In firing at Austria's Ferdinand,
A war that nothing could withstand
Was upon Europe fast unleashed
Destroying a century of relative peace

Save for conflict one on one
Which one country or the other won,
And colonial conflicts far away
Which in distant lands did stay
The cavalry charges in the Crimea
The course of Europe did not steer

Four years of terror in the mud
Bullets, shells and streams of blood
Then when finally, with treaties of peace
Intended to make mass killing cease
There would arise more mighty states
Which lives of millions more would take…

By the same author

Why You Are Here – Briefly

Why am I alive?

To find out why you are alive

What if I don't want to?

Then you won't

And once I find out

New vistas will open

OK, I want to know who I am

Good, you can do that

Really?

Since you don't know who you are

How does that follow

If you already knew, you couldn't find out

…

By the same author

Worry-Free Happiness

Gratitude Golden Syrup

Gratitude is the golden syrup of happiness. When you feel grateful, happiness arises spontaneously, like a bubbling stream.

Here's how to start. As you wake up, give yourself a moment to notice your wakefulness and sense your surroundings. Having done that, express gratitude for the new day. It's a wonderful present.

Stir in the Gratitude Golden Syrup for everything you notice: your eyes, ears, body, the air you breathe, your room and so on. And it doesn't seem to matter who or what you think you are thanking. Gratitude starts your day happy.

Remember the saying: you don't know what you have got until you lose it? Gratitude helps you know what you have got while you have it. Being thankful for life is life-changing.

Happy hint: try gratitude every day for a week, if it works, continue daily.

More titles at Amazon
Verses at Instagram. Follow lightverses
Videos at YouTube
Events at nigellinacre.com

Thanks to
Margaretha Linacre who made it better,
And encouraged me throughout.
Mark Thomason for listening and feeding back,
Sue Linacre and Jac Wilson for final edits.
Big thank you all.

44382403R00076

Printed in Poland
by Amazon Fulfillment
Poland Sp. z o.o., Wrocław